Becoming Adult

Adele Ven

Dedication

To my younger self

because it gets harder

But then it does get better

About the Author

The first book was written by Adele, who had been writing poems and short stories since she was around 11 years old. She currently resides in London with her family, and her book reflects on her atypical childhood, which involved managing both personal challenges and community involvement.

Table of Contents

Wild Times

What wild times to be living in
Being neither here nor there
With a constant of unstable stability
As the only certainty

Being present in body but not mind
Or present in mind but not body
Too busy focusing on the future
To notice current happenings

So much head space taken up
On just getting through the day
All other duties, tasks and chores
Often fall along the sideway

When you say no
But your advocate says yes
When you take on others' responsibility
Just piling up unnecessary stress

Each day becomes an adventure
Every week a mysterious surprise
The month is over without closure
And suddenly another year has gone by

Under the surface not much looks like it's happening
But beneath its actively bubbling
So whilst day-to-day might seem like nothing
With time a whole lot is occurring

And so many days
Bring with them much chaos
The abnormality must now be the stable norm
To help make sense of the fuss

What wild times we must live in
When there's never just one coherent thought
As all the things that must be done
Rush back into the mind as one

Into a space too small to be contained
Hence creativity was named
To bring to life what was inside
And show the world a wild time

Life is Nothing Like a Book

Life is not a book

In its unpredictable way

It's not neatly ordered

But arranged as come what may

A books chapter is but a stepping stone

Part of the bigger picture

Once it is done and dusted

It is never revisited

But oh so no with life

Whose every chapter contains a tale

And when a new beginning arrives

The previous one doesn't ail

There can be multiple stories

All happening at once

Or some you hope have ended

Still spinning you in a dizzying dance

The chapters aren't folded and put aside

They follow you everywhere

On a terribly confusing ride

Confounding all thoughts

Yet still, life must carry on
Pretending all is normal
Trying to make time for inner contemplation
To try and make sense of the situation

Is the subconscious overthinking
Is there internal imbalance
Perhaps there was gut instinct misreading
An inner storm needing to be rebalanced

It's all the chaos combined
That keeps life so interesting
If it were neatly laid out
Then it would be far too boring

Autumn Night

T'was autumnal midnight
And the colours in the sky
Were like a later summer's eve

With the orange of a sunset
Clinging to the clouds
Aroura green shifting in the breeze

The white of early sunrise in the navy blue
The glassy moon
Halfway through
Casting a spotlight in the puffs around
Being admired from the ground

For moments few
The vibrant hues
Then gone without a clue

Save for the lunar glow
The milky clouds
The inky sky
The ashy shrouds

Such events can only be

Found within a city

Where the lights are so bright

They're reflected in the clouds

Unnatural yet beautiful

Subdued yet proud

Because when the silver stars are obscured

By fog or street lights

The artificial is made to be pure

Above the shadows in clear sight

Old Soul

I'm one of those old souls
Who has gone through life many times before
I'm young but not sprightly
Feeling already worn down by life

I'm one of those old souls
Who wants to explore my depths
Not the type that is eager to please
This time I just want to be

I'm one of those old souls
That's aware it's been here before
Full of damage from long-time use
But wholesome at its core

I'm one of those old souls
Who can just sit for hours and ponder
Comfortable to be in a bubble of thought
So different from the rest, full of self-wonder

I'm one of those old souls
Who sort of knows their life's goal
Who understands the struggles to achieve it
And patiently waits for the day it will be whole

At War

I'm in a constant state of war
If I'm not fighting something, it's someone
If it's not someone, it's a fight with me-
My body

Between my nature versus my mind
Because I want to command over it
And it truly commands me
One side is always winning
There is very little middle ground

I feel so out of sync
With everything and everyone
This battle to stay all in one piece
Means conversations that aren't in my head
Are awkward and stiff ones

I can't wait for this war to be over
But there are battles every day
Sometimes there are lapses of tranquillity
Yet those moments are never there to stay

One day I'll meet the conservationist
Whose emotions are satisfyingly deep
We will fight together to put our monsters to sleep

Sweet Memory Shine

The memories are wistful
Flowing with a glittery shimmer
The thoughts are wishful
Wanting to return to the glimmer

'Cause looking back, the sun always shined
Even the snows glittered
A childhood to be mined
Of all the treasures within just littered

And when sweet memory
Crosses with fantasy
It creates a movie in my head
The past is easily misread

That's when I long to reunite once more
To sort the confusion out
Remember my feelings for sure
And leave what was in no doubt

But it's impossible when you can't
And all you can do is wonder
'Cause you're all so far apart
Not allowing confusion to pull you under

One always stays afloat above
Life continues to go on
The sun remains up in the sky
The future is never gone

Although the paths branched away
There's no saying they won't loop back
There's no sanctity and dismay
Depression is not the right tack

So when all is said and done
And the inner battles are won
Remember it's not about the fun
But appreciating the sun
Oh, sweet memory shine on

Comfort

What is comfort?

Comfort is a pillow

Soft and sturdy

That catches my head

And cushions the blow

Comfort is the ground below

The constant stability

On which to roam

A base of security

Some call it "home"

Comfort is knowing

Which path to take

So I don't make a mistake

And suffer another heartache

Comfort is safe

Comfort can be found in hindsight

The realization that it's now all right

To look back at a confusing space

And fit the pieces into place

Comfort is found in familiarity

Which can sometimes prevent destiny

If I find comfort somewhere low

Staying there won't help me grow

Comfort is the know

The place to return

Just like a home

One must leave it to earn

Blind Fire

Full moon, midnight
The forests so bright
Head out for a stroll
To take in it all

Better dispel some dark
Make the contrast more stark
See clearer reach higher
With the aid of fire

With your close circle so strong
You don't notice something's so wrong
Whilst the view around you is major
You could be surrounded by danger

It's always a risk to play around
When you have to rely on just sound
Because beyond the firelight it's blinding
And all you can see is nothing

So before you light up a burning flame
Know nothing will be the same
'Cause it doesn't just help, it hinders
Can easily turn you to timbers

And easily comes the cure

Its source the purest of pure

Past your borders look out

Thy safety shall not be in doubt

The Arches

I see the arches everywhere
Even if they aren't really there
It's the splendour of illusion
The grandeur of confusion

They strike without warning
Night, noon and morning
They don't last for long
And each one has its song

I see the arches everywhere
No two can compare
I often pause as I walk
Too much thinking to do

An arch is but a byway
In which nothing can stay
It is but a traveller's path
Few see the message in its mark

I see the arches everywhere
Some make me stop and stare
For they might just be a means to an end
But are a sign you can always mend

The beauty lies in the wait
The time can change your gait
The travel is the destination
The power of transformation

I see the arches everywhere
A symbol of repair
It doesn't always reach all the way over
For it to feel like it wants you closer

To be wrapped in an embrace
Wearing protections face
As the end draws near
And returns your fear

I see the arches everywhere
For that moment they really are there
Patience lies in corridors long
They appear for me, so to capture them is wrong

I Want You to Know

I want you to know

That I am here for the long haul

Despite the oppression, I will stand tall

I am here to fight to get through

That there is no reconsidering what I plan to do

I want you to know

That I lead my way

I won't blindly do what you say

Being older helps you see my power

But I've been wielding it since before you saw

I want you to know

That despite all this armour

There is a little me sitting below

With the desperation too vulnerable to show

I want you to know

I will not be ignored

This assurance is forever internally stored

I can wait for the day and not get bored

Because I know how to enjoy the tour

I want you to know

That I know too

And precisely what to do

Alpha Female

I've learnt some things about myself recently

Important stuff, like whom I'm meant to be

About where my place is in our society

I feel like I've been given the oversight of a referee

My destiny was born to lead

But differently to the others before me

The calm, strong, waves of authority

Gently and persistently washing over everybody

I want to be respected but not admired

Because tranquillity is what's desired

People will know what has transpired

My impression will hang around, even after I've expired

The type of leader I aspire after

Is able to deal with any disaster

She is not threatened by the rise of those around her

All she wants is to make the pack better

By emanating security to every follower

She is the alpha

An alpha is someone that can carry their own

Who is able to find a place whatever she does roam

Who is able to do just fine all alone

But doesn't compete with the one she calls home

An alpha female's balance is tight

She will <u>not</u> hesitate to stick up for her right

She has an incredibly powerful yet subtle might

Her actions are calculated with plenty foresight

Being an alpha is who I am

So of course my future has way too big of a plan

Through learning all this I now understand

The world is my pack and I have the upper hand

Small Things

I'm not the person I used to be

Nor will I be that way again

It's not a change of negativity

But the way that life presents

What brought about this change?

An understanding of in this trapped world

How to be free range

When the fist of fate is curled

It's the small things, you see

That can make the future look less bleak

When happenstance is so big, so great

The small things take away from the hate

A baby's gurgle as you greet them

A friend's call of support

Those who make you feel special

For being an individual

Taking you away for a little while

Bringing to your face a genuine smile

A song of encouragement
Of faith and acceptance

For daring me to do that which you are too afraid
Telling me after I've done it
And making me feel great

There are also the little things
That remind you life is hard
Those who want you to share all the details
And don't let you get away so fast

The ones who say something insensitive
Whilst trying to get through
Suddenly an expert in all
But don't really know what to do

The small things have changed me
Over time amassing to something great
The small things will continue to be there
To see them take notice they do not wait

The Dating Game

Oh how often it is called a game
But it involves real feelings and blame
People aren't objects made of stone
Their emotions aren't yours to own

So stop messing us about
Let us sort out our confusion and doubt
And once we're sure, don't bully us for more
Because always we're affected to the core

It's a cruel, cruel world don't make it harder
Courage is not something found in the larder
Do you think its easy to put on a brave face?
And pretend like you have your life in place?

It starts with a call, a promising prospect
And is then examined from every aspect
When it is determined they just might fit
It's up to us to decide the final bit

Even though you've been given the green light
Your gut instinct says something just isn't right
So you try again until you know for certain
Leaving the least amount of room to be hurt in

At last this chapter is done and dusted

Or so you thought until your cocoon was busted

They want you to go back, revisit, re-evaluate

As if it's up to them to decide your fate

Didn't they come to the realization?

That you gave this much thought and deliberation?

In cases like these people always get hurt

Not letting dogs lie just makes things worse

Its like you`re the game-makers and we`re the pawns

Unwilling players you`re prodding with thorns

We need our time before making a move

And you want a checkmate quick and smooth

One player makes a move unforeseen

Now the game need never have been

But the game-makers rush to try salvage

That which some might see as garbage

One person's trash is another's treasure

Because we don't all use the same measurer

When you throw it on others do they see its value

Why should I trust you when I have proof not to?

Dating isn't a pastime for fun

There are consequences to every action done

It's not a game you can manipulate

`Cause peoples whole futures are at stake

So if I'm not as docile as you want me to be

Know I won't let my free will be taken from me

Though they might take time, my decisions are final

You can`t so easily get me to spiral

A message to all other people involved

Please keep your distance unless otherwise told

If your input is not requested, please don't deliver

It's difficult enough so cry me a river

I Ask

I ask

Why?

Why does the sun shine so bright in the sky?

Why does time often seem to fly?

Not in the moment but in hindsight

I ask

Why does wisdom

Only come with years?

I ask why I couldn't know more before?

So that I could have achieved more

I ask for it not to be too late

And that I haven't waited too long

To come to my senses and take hold of my fate

I needed to ask

If we could have negotiated things earlier

I needed to ask for help sooner

I needed to ask because I shouldn't have been ignored

I needed to ask many more questions

I needed to ask myself

Many difficult things

But I've been able to find answers

And the wisdom of years

27

Three Words

I will try
Three simple words
Motivation to continue, heart-warming
An attempt at something, life changing

I don't know
Three easy words
A cop-out from either feelings or the truth
And the reason why so many waste their youth

I'll be there
Three heavy words
A promise of commitment, often from the heart
An open invitation from those who are apart

I want to / I need to
Three similar words
One implying selfishness, the other survival
Knowing which to give in to and which is the rival

I'm going to
Three forceful
Words of determination
Reason to continue on, a source of motivation

Away

The future is a dream
I intend to make true
Easing not only my burden
But those of a few

Why is it that it's always away?
And not where we are
That is the place we want to stay
For our origins to be afar

Does physical distance
Make us think it's harder to reach
So we give up on it more easily
Envious of those on the beach

The significance of leaving
Is moving on from my past
Displaying a new era
Because life goes by too fast

The future is a dream
Of me being far away
I can still decide
If it's there I want to stay

Getting Through

I've had some really dark moments
Times when I wanted to give up
When my life felt full of confinement
Every few days feeling I've had enough

Of course, this happens most when I'm alone
Which I am a lot of the time
Sometimes this phrase comes to mind
"I don't want to live but I don't want to die"

So I find things to live for
Making plans that aren't too far in advance
Even my bucket list is a bit of a chore
But there's no quitting before giving it a chance

I want to give up most when I'm lonely
So I need to find things to distract me
I need to find someone to hold me
What I really need most is company

Lately, I've been wishing for the old days
When friendships were so simple
I missed the ease of childhood ways
Even though being a kid was never ideal

I miss the boys who used to be my friends
Because I used to relate better to them
Being a tomboy child there were shared interests
And the most enjoyable conversations we had

Growing up changed all that
As we came into our genders, differences built
Distance came between us hormonally and societally
So useful relationships had to wilt

There were other friendships along the way
Not enough were there to stay
I'm now at the stage for a romantic relationship
But so worn out trying to find a guy who fits

I want someone to look at me
The way guys on-screen look at the girls they love
With this feeling that doesn't go away
That grows stronger and fonder with each passing day
The ones who don't become used to each other
But whose feelings grow deeper the longer they are together

What's interesting about these heavy thoughts
Is very few are about me
It's because I want more for myself
I'm not ashamed of who I am, I'm not a nobody

I believe I was destined for great things
They're just taking a long time to arrive
Though I wait for what each day brings
Some have already been, you don't always see them go by

Many times it doesn't go to plan
So I over think about what to do
I tried to keep in tune with my gut
Follow where my heart tells me to
Good things will come if I wait
Not knowing the future means it can be great

I'm aware there will be hardships ahead
But without the pain it's not worth the gain
So I'll get through day by day
Until the era of peace, where there's plenty more to say

Exasperation

Dear well-intentioned passers-by
Stop telling me that I need a rich guy
I don't have time for your exasperated sigh
That I let great opportunities slip and fly

I know what I want
I know what I need
To tell me I'm dreaming
Won't cause my vision to recede

If you don't ask me first
How will you know?
If you don't know my north
How can you point me where to go?

And for those who are more prominent in my life
What will it take for you to open your eyes?
You can talk and speculate but you still do nothing
We aren't really that close because you didn't do even something

So I will patiently stick and wait
Only because this is my fate
I won't settle for less just because you're late
My future will be better than great

Goodbye Guilt

My guilt is gone
I've got no cares left to give
Like I'm wrung out too much
To feel bad for the things I did

I'm too full with others' stresses
To start carrying my own
So any recent slip-ups
Slide by with a shoulder shrugged "Oh well"

I feel like I'm taking back my own
By not dispensing extra cares
By expressing anger at something else
Instead of swallowing it in my depths

In order to conserve and rebuild
The guilt must go
And it's easier living this way
So why try make that change

Whenever something happens
When the guilt is supposed to come
I feel a sick pleasure from the numb
One less extra worry for this one

Home

There's no place like home
I guess I don't have a place
The terminology thrown about so freely
Calling "home" my base is a disgrace

Home is a place to where you return
For me its a place for which I yearn
Where privacy is a comfort
Not a hideout or deep-etched loneliness

Home is where the heart is
But mine is empty, alone
Too full of the feelings I don't feel
To hold a companion, to let emotions roam

Home isn't a place, it's a feeling
Which explains why I feel homeless
I may have a roof over my head
But the atmosphere is reckless

Home is a shelter from the storms
But when they're happening within the walls
What kind of protection do I get?
Home is where I haven't reached yet

21

Twenty-one
Adulting officially begun
The work is never done
Way overrated is the fun

Twenty-one
The end of young
Childhood far-flung
Ready to be re-sung

Twenty-one
The year for some
When good things come
An annoying hum

Twenty-one
I want to run
From life's cruel plan
Noticed by none

Twenty-one
The weight of a tonne
Heartbreak for one
Of everything undone
Welcome in everyone

The Fight for Justice

So, you want to hear the truth?

Do you want to understand what you know?

Can you be set free by honesty?

Will you stop fighting after justice is served?

Well, let's start at the beginning

In the perfect world of a child

So perfect there are rips in the seams

But of course, they need not know

Until it happens one day

When the world gets torn apart

Buy a stranger's hands in the wrong place

Who should have never been there to start

A catastrophe so great, for years there are no words

Swallowed panic causes disturbances

And the journey to fix up begins

Precautions are the final steps to healing

But the anger burns strong

When the tearing is discovered to have been a bomb

And no amount of combat training

Could ever deal with this problem

So you want to hear the truth?

A stranger has infringed upon the child

In public, with witnesses, who failed to help

And the offender's face had been forgotten

Do you want to understand what you know?

That the life you have experienced

Was actually a great facade

And normal existence is now impossible

Can you be set free by honesty?

Does admitting the past absolve one

By stripping away the mask

Of ever putting it up to begin with?

Will you ever stop fighting after justice is served?

Justice will never be fully served

Until all offenders are punished for their offences

It's for all the vulnerable people

And against those that got away

I am a THRIVER!

I don't want to be seen as a survivor

I'm not a victim, I got past it

But I'm more than just a survivor

Or at least one day I hope to be

To be labelled as a survivor implies

That you're hanging on by a thread

And that each day is a struggle

Because I had a past

I'm more than just a survivor

I am a thriver, a THRIVER!

I took ownership of my life

And precautions against strife

I don't let the past define me

I'm better than my destiny

Don't limit me with a name

Your journey isn't the same

Yes, I had a tainted time

But my future is MINE

Suffering

Do you ever see the good girl

Looking like she's got it all

In appearance and conversation?

But she's silently calling for help

Just like ducks

Swimming so serene

But frantically paddling beneath

Living but not experiencing

Yet what you do feel is loneliness

Even when with friends

When you should be having fun

You're quiet because you don't feel heard

How can you find the words?

Without feeling like you've made a burden of yourself

To tell someone how much they mean to you

And how badly you need their support

But feel like you'll be oversharing

Yet sometimes you just need them

And they're not there

If you tell the truth will you ruin the connection?

Whenever you're in company
You're still alone in your head
Because no one here relates to you
So the bubbly mask is put on instead

And that sweet, good girl
Has it really really hard
And those that know, pretend it's breezy,
Cause she's getting through this so easy.
Yet every smile she displays
Is hiding an angry wave
When it explodes one day
People will say
We never saw it coming our way

Because you didn't know how to ask for aid
And they didn't pick up your pain
So many attempts have gone down the drain
But the goodness is not in vain.

Love

What is love?

Love is innocence

Love is presence

Love is acceptance

   Home is love

Where is love?

Love is everywhere

When you have it

In the greenness of the grass

The brightness of the sky

In the family surroundings

The embrace of friendship

Love is unreachable

When it's not spilling out of you

Beyond the beauty in nature

Past the grasp of home

Everything is a little more dim

It's hard to picture a future that's not grim

Love is a feeling

A force of nature

Love is what endures forever

Love needs to be held
Otherwise, it falls, falls
Away into the abyss
Where everything is amiss

Love is fragile
Love is strong
Love is warm
Love is a song

My heart has been broken
Longer than it was whole
I have no recollections
From when I didn't have a shattered soul

But love is like the gold in the glass
Healing and beautifying the cracks of the past

Love is a gift that grows when cherished
And can make the tough times seem like bliss
It may take a while, but love is a permanent fix

Full Circle Moments

I had a full-circle moment today
As I was taking out my young charges to play
And the grounds were cold and muddy and white
Snowflakes still falling, enhancing the sight

Upon looking around, a sense of completion washed in
The extremism of being here at both ends of the year
When there was grass and leaves and fruits on the trees
To when there was pristine snow, vegetation bare

We're at different points on the circle all the time
They start and go by before it's realized
Till suddenly we meet the end once again
What a small world we're living in

Let What's Done Be Done

It was over two years ago

My mind was so sure then

But they speak to me as if I don't know

And they never let me forget

I don't want to spend another year in this room

The windows open and closed

Heat on and off as cool wind blows

Another summer (single) looms

I don't know whether to be awed or angered

As if this was all meant to be

Or as though I'm being played like a fiddle

And real feelings do not matter

What does matter is anxiety

Wholly consuming me

As I ponder if this is right

Or an out there desperate plea

Surely if it was meant to be

It wouldn't feel like this

Like settling instead of winning

As if I have become the trophy

Why should things be different now?

If I'm the only one who changed

I'm less like what they wanted then

It's less of a fit so why am I always named

What's done has been done

Let the dust remain still

Why stir up what has long been outrun

How long till they've had their fill

I've already said I'm not a piece to be played

So I'll say this one last time

My NO is solid black though you see grey

Hear me

Listen

Understand I don't have the patience of mind

And your intentions are perceived as unkind

Monster of Wrath

I get stuck in my head sometimes
Lost in my inner world
I'm more like my own universe
Having expanded more than one should unfurl

It starts with the story of a little girl
More alert than most it seems to all
And a bigger than-big belittled the small
That's when the balance inside began to swirl

How could a being do a thing so wrong?
How can others stand by and do nothing?
How can someone who used to be the centre-
The pride and joy and grace of the unit
Suddenly be cast to the side lines

How long were you going to pretend?
That it was just a friend
That nothing really happened
How did nobody notice the change?
The shortage of my emotional range

The ignorance, the lack of help, the no understanding
The no exceptions, no sheltering
The not being heard, the lack of justice
The despair

But a child acting on anger gets punished
So away went the fury and out came the smile
Why bother to cry out if it will fall on deaf ears?
So here is Miss Sunshine for the next little while

The internal flame of anger had to be snuffed
So an inside tank was created
To neutralize it so it can`t be felt or seen
But wisps of smoke occasionally escaped

Time went on, things progressed
The little girl saw it with new eyes
She knew: with only one thing are men obsessed
An older self filled in the rest

And as over the years, genuine discrepancies were made
The mishandling of consequences stayed
A thirst for justice from someone so parched
One's own system was invented too harsh

The tank soon became a lake

As the mass within grew and had to suffocate

But then the anger took another take

It learned how to live just great

It was pushed deep, deep down

Sat on by a persona of perfection

It didn't take long to stop gasping and frown

The learning began

Of how to smile through the tears

To push away the frog in my throat

Swallowing it into the pits below

Each one fodder as the monster began to grow

The mass became its own being

Learning to breathe and breed and thrive

Thrashing beneath the surface of the water

That I had no clue was alive

There were times when it would show its face

After being poked and prodded in the wrong place

As if to shout "I'm a contestant in this race"

To then retreat to its numbing embrace

Finally, it was a river
Held back only by a dam
So strong no blow can make it quiver
Yet every injustice tries to ram

Sometimes there's a feeling
Like there might be an explosion
An outburst of frustration
That if let go will send everyone reeling

Sometimes it translates to impulse
To just do something to make an impact
To do something to those who wronged me
A snippet of the justice they deserve
Of the penance they didn't pay
Of the remorse they probably never felt
Of the apologies I never got

Perhaps to do something stupid
To quell the voices within
To satisfy the curiosity of what it would be like
To be seen, and valued, and heard
For my truth to be known

But all I get is a blind eye, a deaf ear
Seen only for what I don't want to be seen
My surface, temporary worry, fake me
Not the lonely, hurt, inner me

When the attention given is to satisfy themselves
Not to genuinely query about wellbeing
When someone else benefits more than me
Thinking they know better when they aren't seeing

I was the centre of it all
'Till one day it was taken away
I always knew it wasn't my fault
No one seemed to get it and I forgot to scream

The sea is now draining from its chasm
As the tears that filled it slowly shed
All the energy going to healing the gash
Which grew wider with every lack
But the scar is still a striking black
Spreading quickly like a rash

As the level drops, the pain rises
Often becoming outraged by surprises
Not people learnt from their ways
And are now doing better
But it was all denied me back then
It's not fair those who deserve it less
Get it much quicker

The monster adapts easily

Underwater or dry land

It wants me to act

Everyone was wrong so on my own I stand

Quick and cruel

Make right fast what was done wrong in the past

No mercy on account of no compassion

Try not to let common sense ration

The volcano needs an outlet

Or it threatens to explode

The pain needs a voice

Or the future could implode

Wrath shalt run free within me

Waiting for the day it will show no mercy

Stuck

I saw my life stretched before me
All its potential and all my years tied
Where I was now wasn't where I wanted to be
And I felt stuck

Doors would open freely
The feeling of changes to come
But it wasn't happening fast enough
And I felt stuck

The last years of school dragged away
Yet somehow flew and next I knew
That hurdle was overcome
Still, I felt stuck

I was unsatisfied with just one job
So I added on another
It didn't help quite enough
And I still felt stuck

Yet recently something changed
The antsy feeling diminished hurriedly
Ironically, I'm truly stuck now
But I've never felt freer

Before things were moving at a snail's pace
I felt stuck
Now things are at a standstill
I feel free

I was waiting for things to happen
Feeling helpless to push things along
I didn't understand and it was frustrating
I was stuck in that cycle

Felt like I had no routine
Even though there was a schedule
Now, life is at a standstill
But I feel loose

I used to shut myself away
Finding no respite for the need to be out there
Time was going too fast but life too slow
I realized it was my feelings that were stuck

Now the whole world is shutting down
I should be feeling more bound than ever
Instead I see opportunity to be
I'm at peace with this break

It's as if I've been given the gift of time
To be, to heal, to see
To gaze afresh upon the world
And feel its colour and majesty

The dam is open
And I have time to run free
Then get back in control of myself
Before it's time to face the world again

Maybe this is just a respite
And the feeling will come back soon
But I'll try keep a hold with all my might
Whilst moving fast, seeming to do nothing
And the future won't wait until noon

The Death of My Friend

A great friend passed away today
I don't know what to say
I kept uttering no no no
And let the tears flow and flow

My heart started pounding
Waiting to hear it wasn't true
But only messages of condolences
Kept coming through

What do I do now?
How am I supposed to feel?
This grief feels beyond me
The downs of life are far too real

The guilt that I heard others talk of
Has visited me now
Why didn't I do more?
As if I could have helped somehow

It doesn't weigh me down
Just runs around in my head
I should have been a better friend
But she is one word: dead

Such a mighty gut-punch

Delivered with so few words

My feelings are fighting with me

They can't be pushed down

They must be heard

To make things even worse

The emptiness of no one to talk it through

I can't process this alone

Or choose the wrong person to turn to

I'm oh so sad

But oh so glad

I processed with my cry

There are still tears in my sigh

I bid her a final goodbye

At Times I Feel

At times I feel

When there's nothing else to do

Emotion must come through

One moment there here

The next moment they're gone

At times like these I feel sad

The grief comes charging forward

Such a short funeral

I couldn't cry properly then

At times I feel nostalgic

Living in memories

Stirring up happenings past

Evoking rose-coloured nostalgia

Or long-forgotten anger

And then I let my thoughts stew

At times I feel numb

Because there are too many feelings

And giving in to them means I will succumb

So they all get pushed far away

Then I wonder why I've got nothing to say

Because I wished it all away

Too far, because I can never get them to stay

But in times like now

A constant feeling permeates

I'm feeling down

That's okay for now

Right now I feel

Like I've never felt before

All these new feelings

Have uprooted my core

And I'm emotionally sore

Surfing the Waves

Survey the vast sea

Stretching out all around thee

Too great to be contained

All on its own maintained

Remark upon each wave

Arising of its own accord

Gathering momentum in the wind

Becoming too strong to rescind

With however much power got stuck on the thought

The wave will grow equally tall

Higher and higher, crescendo, pause

Then down with a crash and a mighty roar

Feel the power that pulses through

Thy knows not what to do

To be pummelled underwater as each wave breaks

Crushed by the consequences of mistakes

A tug coming from down below

Is the reach of salvation too far to go?

A cord of life, black against the blue

Opportunities for life are so few

If thoust was able to pull it nearer

Hope becomes ever clearer

Use the last reserves to hop on the board

Survival chances are now restored

Floating aimlessly no land in sight

Giving up just isn't right

Slowly and steadily take a stand

Surfing the waves is mighty grand

And the waves will still come

In varying sizes of tall

Thy tether is strong so you can get back up

Every time you fall

Survey the vast sea

Resting there so calmly

But you've ventured into its midst of shallows and depths

Surfboard underfoot there's much to be discovered yet

What I Say vs What I Mean

Often in conversation, I find myself
Saying one thing but meaning something else
Or saying just a little when there's much more
People think I'm quiet coz they don't see beneath the fore

When I say "I'm fine" or "I'm okay"
90% of the time I'm not, I'd rather you go away
Because no one really wants to be there
I'd rather be satisfied pretending to care

When I say "I don't need anything/I'm good"
It means something is needed but I don't trust you could
Better to spend time in solitude than in inferior quality
If I can't hold your full attention why should it be me?

When I say "I don't know" in answer to a complex question
Often I do know but can't find the words to fit my conviction
Or my mouth has answered before I've had a chance to think
Before a decent response comes up, the conversation moves on in a
blink

When I say "there's nothing I can do"
Quite often there is, it's just not legal to
Sometimes the actions necessary are well beyond my means
So I mutedly back away and do it in my dreams

The Road

Behold the treacherous road

So worn from many a traveller

There is nary in sight an abode

Upon which to rest for even an hour

The paving has come away

So there is no distinguishing line

Between pedestrian and vehicle

Between safety and danger's vine

Everyone starts out alone

Until others make themselves known

To show them how to do it on their own

So they can pass it all on when they've grown

Sometimes they don't show up

Until it's almost too late

When the damage has been done

Only help can change their fate

The superficial is easier to deal with

To make a big fuss over and sort

But the underneath is still left in turmoil

There is not yet aid for the distraught

To simply trim the weeds

Is pretty much moot

If they are not removed

By pulling them up by the roots

When the road does cross

A new untrodden path

Full of vegetation and the unseen

At any moment a new danger's chance

Behold the treacherous road

Its pitfalls are known by now

There are others to guide you through

And you can add on to the next time they endow

Light

At the end of the tunnel is light

But it was midnight

The moon a shrivelled slice

No help in sight

When the only way out is through

But there's no glow to guide you

Which direction does one choose?

Without knowing whether they've turned back or chosen true

Is this a nightmare or silent screams?

Memories or lucid dreams?

Has the darkness induced the doubt?

Was the goal always to just get out?

The tunnel seemed so inviting at first

Daylight growing adventures thirst

So in one goes as the sunset gives a wink

Then it disappears before the comprehension of a blink

Keep walking forward

The motto to go by

Tripping, spinning, falling in the darkness

Then which way to try

Follow the tracks

Hold steady the wall

Breathe in the discovery

The joy of learning to wherewithal

In the tunnel of life

It is others who light our way

When a torch beam isn't enough

Spotlights of aid light our way

They are sight to the blind

The definition of kind

They make one want to reach the end

Not stay stuck in the throughway

Convinced the walls are a friend

To reach the air, the breeze, the trees

To feel the accomplishment and peace

No matter if its day or night

When you get out, there is always light

Full and Empty

Every day brings with it a new opportunity

A chance for healing

A space for old wounds to be sealing

Time for the future's unveiling

Right now, I feel surprisingly whole

Like my weekend was a balm for my soul

Whilst the craving for touch still lives on my skin

Inside the necessary affections did win

It's weird to feel so complete

Yet like a black hole at the same time

As I have realized best in myself to retreat

And the maternal caring is an extra sublime

Being full and empty

Simultaneously

Knowing for the meanwhile

This is how it's going to be

Better like this

Then a complete abyss

Filled by caring

Empty from oversharing

Orphan

I feel like an orphan
Whose parents happen to still be alive
Lacking parental attention
And the innocence needed to thrive

I'm a piece of the family's crumbly pie
A bunch of parts squished together
An image of completeness that's a total lie
But my crumbs seem to be a different colour

Apparently I never knew my mother
Only a shadow of who she once was
I never had much of a father
And every day I live with the loss

To my plight everyone is blind
Because my circumstance is of the wrong kind
And I appear to be like everybody else
All deaf to my (not so) silent cry for help

I live in a house that's never been a home
Hoping someday to grow one of my own
But if I am unseen, it might as well be a dream
Someone like me, living in the middle of a close-knit community

Stay

To the one whom I hold dear
I know we're in rough times
Still, I long for you to be near
Don't want the past to reprise

When at first you were there all the time
But as was natural, that changed
And as I enter my prime
We are becoming estranged

Things were so difficult before
When it felt like I was on my own
Then things seemed to restore
And I no longer felt so alone

When you were gone
The words went too
All tied up with nothing to draw on
There was very little I could do

When you slowly began to come back
Things were not how they used to be
There wasn't enough of you to fill your lack
The instability of uncertainty

And so, to you

The one who might hold dear

I need you to stick around

And not give in to the fear

Though the future is uncertain

There must be some way to share this burden

In these tough times I wish you would stay

Can you get through without pulling away?

I need to hold on to this closeness we have

No one seems to know or understand

It seems like nothing has gone to plan

There's nobody left to hold my hand

And right now I need to hold on to you

Things can't go back to when you weren't there too

So please don't go

Don't let the past steal the show

The Office

Day in, day out (occasionally out)
Be sure to come diligently in
So that you can sit about
Monotonously doing nothin'

Very excitingly, I'm all alone
So I can get up to stuff
That no one but me knows
So the boredom isn't so rough

In a place like this
Who needs a brain?
The sameness of everything
Can drive you insane

And you live strictly by Murphy's Law
When suddenly there's an influx of calls
Annoyingly, they're not spread out more
There's a work overload and you didn't catch them all

The skills needed here are so few
My brain feels tired from lack of use
Time to draw on creativity
To find something to do

Overall, its wasted time well spent

And the money each month

Is more than just a dent

So I'm off to continue doing nothing

Eventually

It's about more than just the money

But stimulation and fulfilment

So, I know, one day I will go

But not just yet

Got to really make sure

There's nothing to do in the nothing time first

Death

We all die at some point
Some sooner than others
It doesn't matter if we are ready
Before death comes to take us

Each day we are closer to the day we meet him
Death toys with us in circles
So we should constantly be on our toes
In case he pounces unexpectedly and all goes dim

Sometimes he comes too close for comfort
So that we are forced to stare him in the face
Few are able to turn him down when he beckons
The rest left behind have to deal with the shake

Many times death arrives too soon
Less than half the people he takes are actually old
He makes us sway to his gut-wrenching tune
Death has taken his role and become too bold

So many have gone far too young
Wasn't the elderly enough?
Are youthful souls a kink to him?
Noble, devastating, master of death do you have to be so rough?

Life is a play and death is our exit
No matter how important, roles always end
It's just a question of how he does it
Will it be expected, or a sudden new trend?

Some people are able to take a bow
Others have time to leave with a wow
Many go with a "does it have to be now?"
More depart before they've ever had a sweat on their brow

Death resides above us all
Though he`s terribly busy trying to be amongst us here
So successful is he, we watch out for his call
Sometimes I wonder if he`s mistakenly taken some overall

To you, master of death
Who leaves more questions than rests
Why can't all young grow old?
How many stories have you stopped from being told?
Does your visit always have to be so painful?
Is all your work merit, or is some of it sinful?

Days Gone By

T'was a warm weekend afternoon
The sun was out, the fields in bloom
So out we went to enjoy the weather
And lounge in the gloriousness of each other

We were younger then
Still in teenage hood, unknowingly zen
And we found the perfect spot to bask
To relax in the sun and the fresh scent of grass

How lovely it was to be
Living in the moment, her and me
Talking about that and this
Other times in silence, in the sound of nature's bliss

The day came and went
I spent more summer days with my friend
We stayed close as time went by
Though through COVID our youth did fly

Being young adults, life was hard
Meeting the harsh world, growing apart
Still keeping in touch, doing more mature things
And discussing stresses and worryings

Suddenly one day

It was all taken away

I wish time I could rewind

'Cause she left us all behind

After, one warm afternoon

When the flowers were starting to bloom

I visited the spot where we once lay

Appreciating the sun and grass and company

How lonely it was to be

Living in this moment overcome with grief

Talking to myself about that day long ago

And there is still so much I don't know

Back then we would speak of the future

Trying to figure it out was a blunder

The twists and turns are too unforeseen

All I can do is speculate about what might have been

Away at Last

I'm finally here
The beginning of my future
The one I dreamed of
And planned for

I've managed to get away
From the place full of sorrows
Into the land of sunshine
Full of adventure

I haven't planned each day yet
Every day brings its own
The lack of structure is healing
I don't feel so alone

From the crowded market streets
To the quiet suburb home
The travels and relaxations
Greater family and friends long known

This time brings a different flavour
The chance to find my lighter part
Many more moments to savour
The taste of leaving behind my past

A New Summer

My favourite summer
That's what this year will be
It's far from over
But the one in charge is me

I've travelled a great distance
To take over myself
Now there is less resistance
In attaining emotional wealth

The past has left me broken
And wired up all wrong
I'm healing in the present
So the future's bright and strong

I haven't been alive that long
But already I feel worn and old
This is the year I reclaim my youth
And enjoy being young and bold

My favourite summer
That's what this year will be
Full of sun and adventure
Becoming the best me

How to Help?

It's fascinating how one issue

Get pushed under the rug

With unfelt words of sympathy

Real offers of help-far and few in between

Suddenly there's an easier problem

And the calls come rushing in

Offers of assistance from everywhere

But they are not needed for this

"Is there anything I can do to help"

No, not the kind you're offering from far away

Because that problem is sorted and won't stay

But that thing living under the rug

Your assistance could be a bear hug

Please don't refuse or ignore

Just say there's nothing you can do anymore

Let me know you're limited but you know someone who can

Don't leave me alone to stand

Of course, my dignity will never let me ask

So please help me out with this simple task

It comes from a place so young and weak

Where human touch is all I seek

The dire need to be comfortingly close

To someone who cares

I cherish it most

A New Beginning

Something has shifted within
I came back ready for things to begin
And start they did, not yet paused
Welcomingly arriving through life's bright doors

It's one thing after another
And my time is pleasantly chill
Reunited with sister and brother
The contentment of an upward hill

I'm falling back in love with life
As my days start to fill and fulfil
My hope has been revived
Knowing more strengthens my will

The extra pep in my step
Is more reason to keep saying yes
And the opportunities now coming through
Are abundance to put imagination to the test

The Spiral

It all started way back when
When I was taken for a spin
Thoroughly shaken disoriented and stumbling
Right into a spiral

Then it was hard to stand straight
Almost impossible to move forward
And it is when you're stuck in a circle
Going round and round to where it all started

I must have stopped spinning long ago
But I'm still deeply twisted
It seems like I haven't recovered at all
Because dizzy and reeling separated

And when the spiral is all you see
It appears to be the path
Till your eyes are opened to it
But you're too entangled in the force

So off the spiral
On to a merry go round
Learn how to navigate still in the wild
Continuously turning, the world profound

It's that first leap of healing

When everything slows down

And you can live in some moments

As you slowly turn around

There is still a long while

Until one will be at a halt

Maybe it won't ever fully stop

Too far from the edge to drop

Doubts

Mixing family and friends
A thing to recommend?
In a gathering is great
But to mess around with fate?

What if things go wrong?
Because something is pushing me away
But if it goes on for too long
Will I feel obligated to stay?

On paper, it adds up
The circumstances are great
It feels too precious to tell
But am I making a mistake?

I keep building it up in my head
Planning the future with him
Like maybe I can see this going somewhere
But something is making it dim

Time will tell
What will be will be
Now, I just have to wait and see

The Date

Twas the end of a very long day
And the dramas would not go away
Time to go meet a potential mate
And figure it out with the date

Walking together through the street
Not worried about who I would meet
Why should there be anything wrong
With two people getting along?

Went to the place I've been in dreams
Together, at night, a lovely scene
I never thought it would actually come true
Childhood imaginings coming to life are so few

It was pleasant building up a rapport
Of topics to speak I wish there were more
It's the little things though that make or break
I sincerely hope I'm not making a mistake

Said goodnight
Suddenly the future seems so bright
The evening is done with a satisfied sigh
And the parting tonight wasn't a goodbye

First of My Kind

I'm different from the others

Even way back then I knew

It's something very few understood

I carried it with me as I grew

To me, things are mostly black and white

I gravitate towards what is right

Most of my life has been spent in the night

But I'm starting to reposition the spotlight

I'm the centre of my own world

Not part of the side-lines of someone else

I'm reclaiming my destiny

Not the bleak image once painted before me

It started when I was young

When I lost hold of a mother's touch

That was always there but just beyond reach

Comfort and belonging were all I did seek

Those around me seemed to have no clue

The pretence of normalcy as I grew

So was the routine even I didn't need convincing

Outside showing a pattern of excelling without trying

When you're young, hardships are greater if you're smart

Because academics is not the place to start

Neither the known apparent social struggles

The real solution -parental cuddles

It seemed to be

That only I saw the star in me

I watched my life from afar

Devoid of emotion to prevent a scar

Since it was all about my way

I didn't care what others had to say

Always awaiting that time up ahead

When I'll be free and emotionally fed

I did think that was small to others

To me, they were big accomplishments

I plan one day to do great things

Starting now before the complications tomorrow brings

The star power I have is undefined

Locked in this powerhouse so refined

This difference in me can teach others greatly

I hope to be the first of my kind

Is Full Whole?

Right now, I feel full
Satisfied
I'm in the right time
Usually, I feel like a black hole

Right now I'm looking forward to:
A future with company
Filled with sun and laughs
Being my best single self
That makes me feel full.

It's easier to picture in these days of sunshine
And very early spring in the air
I am filled with good feelings
Almost till I'm bursting

I still get saddened
By the spaces in my heart
Old and especially new.
Even though I recently suffered a loss
The forever-empty feeling didn't jump out
What is it that I actually feel?

Is this feeling happiness?
This fullness, contentment

Is this what it's like to feel whole?
Or am I just satisfied with where I am
The love and joy and friendships
That makes me feel heard, seen, and wanted
These make me whole

So if I am whole, am I still not full?
If I am full, am I still not whole?
I know I don't have everything to complete me
Does that mean then that I'm simply full?
I feel empty, as a result of gaps within
Are full and whole the same?

To sum up, I feel complete
Better yet-wholesome
I'm full but still empty
I'm whole but still broken
I'm experiencing what it will be like
When one day I am truly whole
I feel wholesome!

Most Happy

I am most happy when

I'm with my family and part of a whole

I am with my network of support and

The focus is on the light

I am most happy when the sun shines

And the future holds something bright

I am most happy when I can plan for a good time

When I can give up control and be shown

I am most happy when I am myself

When I'm free as a bird and I believe

I'm flying, not being weighed down by caring

How Can You Know?

How can you know?

If he is right for you

When there are so many competing feelings

To sort through

When at first you were so drawn in

Ready for the next chapter to begin

But then are you bored or calm

Wanting to leave at the end, is that an alarm?

When they threaten they might say no

Because it's not going fast enough

But its actually a relief if they do

Except you don't want to be the one rejected

But when you think you know

What happens then?

When you're not ready to announce it yet

Because the progression fills you with dread

The next steps take so much planning

So many complex details to work out

With an unknown timeframe

That's what you're stressing about

To figure it out third party
Or directly
Face to face is easier
But will it provide enough solutions

So the light becomes heavy
Defeating the purpose of fun
Really it can come after
And be a bit less of a disaster

Heartache

The tears don't cease their flow
The sky is crying alongside the scene below
This feels like a pain I know
That I was getting over, a year ago

Was this even worth fighting for
If the odds all seemed to be against me
Was it the universe's way of saying
This just wasn't meant to be?

Now I mourn the loss of a future
That had so much promise in store
It was something I looked forward to working on
But I feel shaken to my core

I'm grieving for what we could have had
And for the way in which it ended
For the feelings I thought would never come
Yet finally thought I felt it for someone

I know this pain will pass
Its hard while it lasts
It hurts even more
Not being able to talk

He will always have a place in my heart

For everything I learned about myself with him

Though now we must be apart

We have both grown in the interim

I can't believe it is over

Just like that

And I feel so broken

How can I face the world?

We'll see one day in the future

That we really weren't meant for each other

Losses

There have been several losses

In the recent past

There's opportunity to recast

The roles are vast

I lost my future with a boy

A boy whom I was willing to marry

So bad I wanted to hold his hand

Perhaps a man who can plan, and understand

I lost the vision of the one in my head

A quick look through pics was enough said

Goodbye inner child and her friend

Better find someone who actually exists to pretend

I lost my close friend

For her, it was the end

The gap for you is still open

At least its easier for people when I say I'm broken

I lost my knack for song writing

I hope this one will come back

Now that I have an opening to the field

My abilities should get back on track

I lost my patience

To deal with other people's (blank)

Whether its opinions, "helpfulness" or mind play

Hopefully this one won't come back

Evolving

It began with a splitting
From child to adult-in-training
That was the beginning
Of evolving

There were phases of learning
And relationship configuring
A change of schooling
Finding acceptance was character building

First experiences solo travelling
Finding independence freeing
Being noticed as a woman causes fleeing
The beginning of disordered breathing

Back in the childhood house, living
Discovering the balance of working
The process of healing
After a fresh round of grieving

Then came dating
Bringing self-awareness and maturing
Coming to terms with adulting
Seeing beauty emerge with evolving

Winter Break

It began at dawn
Before the first signs of morn
As the sun, we rose
And slipped into a doze

Descended into afternoon light
The scenery a breath-taking sight
The air so inviting and warm
It's a wonder people don't swarm

A three-day luxurious stay
The peace of being away
There was a lovely city to explore
So much joy in finding more

We ate supper on the beach at sunset
Admiring oranges, yellows, pinks and reds
With views of palms, grass, sands and rocks stretched
A glorious bridge- ancient, worn, yet strong, impressed

How lovely it was to be free

Which made it easier to breathe

And allow the warmth to melt the stress away

Feeling so youthful and at play

99

I will be going back one day

Two Paths

Two people
Same choice
One will be confused
The other will rejoice

All her friends and family gather round
Her decision has made them proud
They congratulate and cheer
As the woes of singlehood disappear

Now it's all about thinking ahead
How to set up a home
The kind of life that will be led
A bright orderly future sweet as honeycomb

At the same time, the same city
For another, this wasn't meant to be
Instead, there were tears and heartbreak
The dismay of others and a new kind of ache

Now it's all about thinking ahead
Finding reasons to get out of bed
As the river of life continues to flow
It cannot be stopped by a dam of sorrow

The months go by
For each of them fast
One is full of anticipation
One is healing from her past

The day of the celebration arrives
It goes precisely as prescribed
Into the deep-end they dive
Two people starting out their new lives

They are blissfully happy
In the way newlyweds tend to be
Finding fulfilment in each other
As they build a home together

And not that far away
An evolving girl finds her forte
She is stronger than ever
Resilience has created a myriad of colour

Due to an open mind
Others respond in kind
New connections are formed
A greater barrier against the storms

The prospect of a different open door

That could never have happened before

It brings a mountain of motivation

This exciting new vocation

Things seem to fall into place

Each day becoming easier to face

In her general appearance it shows

Fulfilment has made itself known

Two people

One day they cross paths

Going about their schedules

Content and continuing past

Someday

The choice will come around again

This time it's a joyful day

It's ultimately a double win

For whilst there is now a new partner

And the future they'll create

There is gratification aside from each other

That made it worth the wait

Helpless

How much do I have to beg?

How much do I have to plead?

What will it take to make you realize?

Few people need you as much as me

Why is it that when I finally cry?

It's out of frustration and not sorrow

Without help how can I continue

How can I face the prospect of tomorrow?

I need you to hear the words I don't say

The ones that I can't verbalise

The ones that are too desperate to be defined

With requests that I don't recognise

Is the mask of age too big to see

The child behind it that is me?

As small and helpless as can be

Stuck in this eternity

It took so long to admit

I can't do this alone

That giving up on my dreams is not the answer

I don't have to do this on my own

Inner Torment

I feel like I want to bash my head in
To make the voices go silent
To stop the jitters and whirling
Maybe embrace the black unconscious

I want to slip there to get some escape
To potentially get clarity
To give up control of my fate
Maybe admit weakness by allowing a faint

The thought of returning is so morbid and grim
Though perhaps it was all packed away as dim
All think they know better about myself
Makes me second guess and doubt the past

I need to bang my head still
To make it stop twisting inside
To stop my thoughts repeating themselves
Maybe put a pause to this wild ride

I hold the power in this situation
The results lie with me
With just a few short words
I can change my reality
And I can't handle that

Not a Doubt

Its been so long

What's pulling me back now?

Have people finally got under my skin

Or am I ready to go back in?

What happened to all the ick?

The discomfort of the idea of this

Does going for this mean I'm settling?

Or am I just now realizing?

That the answer was there all along

It just needed time to form

Is this maturity?

Why does it have to be so messy?

But then the ick came back

Along with the fury and frustration

Why can't they see?

I know what's best for me

It's a chapter that should be closed

Astounding how others don't see

What once might have worked in theory

Is now too different to be

The Lines

These lines
The marks of pain and suffering
So deeply etched
Scars of past outlined

Echoes of stories untold
Of drastic measures of release
When it was all too much to hold
Of sacrificing blood for peace

Each line a torrent of tears
As the emotional torment temporarily eases
There will be freedom in the coming years
Though not in the throes, when time seems to freeze

And the lines remain
When the mind is sane
Reminders of the pain
Now they're dents of disdain

These lines
Are symbols of resilience now
A path to the other side
To where balance resides

Longing

Can you long for someone you haven't met?

It's the void filled by the one, but you don't know them yet

And when you're lonely they get in your head

You start to wonder where they are now, in bed

What if at some point you've already met the one?

But didn't know it back then, you were just out to have fun

And you were close, then grew apart then moved away

Only after some part of you realise you wanted them to stay

So when the time comes for the life partner search to begin

All the effort met over and over with chagrin

The inevitable thoughts make themselves known

How you may have left the one free to roam

As longing deepens your mind turns and tumbles

Your imagination takes over as innovation rumbles

Perhaps a chance meeting, one final conversation

Or possibly the start of an eternal connection

Is it someone I knew or someone I've yet to meet?

Is it possible to tell from a glance on the street?

Do you believe in love-at-first sight or doing what's right?

What if they are the one but now display deal-breaking behaviour?

Are you pining away for the one to be your saviour

They need to be more than just a means of escape

Better to be healed and not rely on them to close the gate

All the easier to move forward quicker

Maybe the longing is a sign that its time

To finally meet and move forward into optimal prime

But until then, all one can do is wish

And hope it won't be too long before they enter bliss

A Dream of Blood

Am I holding onto something

That I know deep down won't last?

Thinking there's a future in us

Because he might be someone I don't want to move past

These feelings of loss and pain

Are being held off

With the hope of reconciling again

Because maybe he can be enough

Am I selling myself short?

By settling for the first one

Even my dreams concur these thoughts

That I mourn though it's not technically over

There are blood stains on the carpet

The stains are deep emotional scars-

I start to feel things once more

And the pain returns and floods my heart

The blood on the floor

Someone might be trying to deceive me

I'm now distrustful of those I know

The old and the new

I don't know what to do

If I'm moving on in my sleep

But awake I say it's not over

Do I know the truth down deep?

And I just don't want to see it

The time will come soon

For the final meet up

And there might be a goodbye

But my feelings don't let me decide

A Beach Day

Sun-kissed
Warm tingly skin
Waves coming in
Soothingly crashin'

There's a harsh line of black
Between the blue and steel-grey
Greyed-out mountains on the horizon
A lovely spot to get away

Sand between toes
The pleasantest of woes
And solid stones
Giving grounding tones

The breeze comes and goes
The end of summer shows
A final day of bliss
Before autumnal storms hit

Seagulls soaring overhead
Starlings strolling nearby
Close enough to stroke
Then its time to bid goodbye

The Land Of The "Free"

The land of the free

Is not a democracy

Its an economy

Where the big dream is money

That is what governs their diversity

The land where they think of nothing else

Except for themselves

And how deep they can sew their pockets

To store their bulging wallets

Most people have money

But it doesn't stretch very far

Most of it is claimed by the government

Under the guise of helping its fallen stars

Born on the ground, never taught to shine

Nothing more than specimens in data jars

And so money

Becomes their priority

Over their families

Because they believe it will make them happy

Though it leaves them without a community

Whether or not they succeed

They are technically "free"

To do as they please

Though not much can be done autonomously

The "free" have to rely on transport

Because it's not feasible to travel on foot

The quantities consumed are so great

People find it difficult to self-regulate

They cling to weaponry

As if to a crutch

If they would know leaving go would decrease mortality

Would they still covet it so much?

It seems that democracy

Has taken this land too far

It is now a monetary, marshal society

But to a "freeman," that idea would appear bizarre

The Scene

A cosy kitchen

A quiet night

The kids are asleep

Time for frivolity

Out come the bowls and mixers

Out comes the list of ingredients

Sugar, flour and moments of laughter

Add a little of this

Sprinkle some of that

Whisk carefully to create the perfect mixture

Portioned out in dainty measure

But in the midst of all the laughs

A wistful thought came to pass

What if my companion was my other half?

Quite similar the scene would be

The atmosphere light and airy

Would the joy be more deep?

Would the night have ended in greater mischief?

All those moments that didn't stay

All those moments of potential foreplay

All those moments flew away

The "can you pass me this"

The "look before you miss"

The cheeky inviting smiles

The philandering of all styles

There may have been a food fight

Laughing way into the night

And the vision ends just right

Morning comes and with it a gleam

A sparkling kitchen

A hectic routine

And delectable edibles as the story its seen

This is in my future one day

I'll make it happen

For the one who chooses to stay

On The Street

They walk down the street

Hands intertwined

Not noticing those they meet

And empty are mine

Their eyes are interlocked

As they share a quiet moment

Leaning forward in closeness

My eyes move onward

I see flowers in the meadow

I put one in my hair

Enjoying bare feet on the grass in sunlight

And wish a special someone was there

It's a warm summer's afternoon

Perfect for a picnic for two

Almost a second honeymoon

Going with a friend just won't do

On a lonely walk in the marsh

I put him facing me

So we can have a conversation at last

On why he hasn't come to be

And he has that look in his eyes
Of focus, of closeness, slightly glassy
With a joy and wanting, gratitude and clarity
It's a forever love that belongs to the wise

This feeling which I've never owned
Yet so many have it who are far less grown
Those people are everywhere I go
In their own little bubble where everything is slow

Where does one find a significant other?
When does it become worth the bother?
Is a love like this not meant for me?
Is to observe other couples my destiny?

In due time I surely will be
Held by strong arms, grounding security
Each morning waking up to you is a treat
And we'll be just like the others on the streets

My arm wrapped in yours
So our strides are part embrace
We'll be chatting merrily, easily
Eyes locked on the others face

Twenty-Two

Twenty-two
Is here at last
Its greatness come true
A victory over the past

I thought twenty-two
Would never come for me
Moments of joy were so few
But plenty more have come to be

And so twenty-two
Is but another step along the way
Ushering in something new
The welcomed arrival of a fresh day

More Precious and Meaningful

What if my life were more precious and meaningful?

Would I have different values from the ones I have now?

Would I want to be more sheltered?

And would I have acted in the greater good in the past?

If my life were more precious and meaningful

I would find more things to fill up my time

I would act more ambitiously,

And not let fear of embarrassment hold me back

Persistence would achieve

I would do things more completely

And put in more soul

Meaning would come from worthwhile things

Nature would be excellent company

Emotions would be heightened

And I would find ways to enjoy the alone

Perhaps I might know more

Or be content with knowing less

I might be more cautious

And I might risk to arrive at my best

It Gets Better

Hello little one, suffering there

Musing in the depths of despair

When there seems to be a lack of those who care

And the cards of life seem so unfair

Feeling so displaced

With many bases yet no home

Her heart striving to be in three places

To make up for being so alone

Each night before falling asleep

Wanting to cry from the pain

Knowing it won't accomplish anything

So the tears don't rain

She asks, will it always be like this?

How many loved ones must I miss?

I picture the future a bleak abyss

Does it get better from this?

So I tell her

Yes it does get better

Many places become few

And home is something new

The suffering eases
Though the cards still come tough
They are easier to manage
After having been so rough

And though there's no other
Lonely doesn't hit so sharp
You made peace within yourself
To work on creating your mark

People will come into your life
Bringing light along the way
A rekindling of connections
That are welcome to stay

So, to me of the past
It gets better as you go
There's support and presence
And wonderful people you get to know

The future looks ripe with growing opportunities
That are beginning to formulate
For work that is tough but good
And not as hard when you know the could

Yes it seems to be so dark

As everything you built falls apart

When one has lost so much

That's a stronger foundation for a new start

It has gotten better

Things are only looking up

And I'll let you know in a few more years

Just how good it's got

I Changed Because

I changed because

The world was changing too

I changed because

I learned different ideals from what I was told to do

I changed because

The world was too cruel

And I wasn't sheltered enough from it

I changed because

I found people who were kind

And always had the best interests in mind

I changed because

Of those who inspired me

About how good of a place this world can be

If each person made an effort or three

I changed because

There was growing to do

Time didn't stand still as I went through

I changed because

A different side of life arose

And I had to deal with the throes

The Dating Cycle

Once again the time has come

When one must and mustn't be numb

To go out and be in touch with one's feelings

And hope they are not misleading

Try and keep light the heavy heart

Open it gently so it won't fall apart

Though it would rather stay shut whilst the mind is on edge

To follow the logic it does pledge

There are so many signs, but what do they mean

Is this just another cycle on repeat?

If this is for nought I want to run away

If this is forever it should be easier to stay

They all couldn't get enough of me before

That has now changed as I am restored

Perhaps I now come across as more healed and healthy

The disinterest that they cannot play around with me

Whether or not this is meant to be

Its what this journey leaves to see

Why is this neutrality so heavy?

Is that good, bad, a sign or a plea?

And so the cycle ends again

Leaving drudgery to set in

For it will repeat, inevitably when

The dizzying dance will once more spin

The stops and starts are wearying

There is no end in sight

To reach the future I'm envisioning

Seems less and less like a journey

And more and more like a fight

Hallows

Oh the irony
Of everything around me
To see the sign
"It doesn't have to be goodbye"
When that's exactly what will be

Over the next months or years
There is an aura of solemnity
For what we had is moving on
And now so must we
This coming on slowly yet abruptly

Now we all grieve
Before they're gone
In our own way

How do you let go?
Of someone you didn't get to really know
Who has been in the background most of the time
And now you have to say goodbye

And death has come

To laugh at me again

Because his work is in the order of things

But he's let chaos go first and is waiting in the wings

So the end will have a deathly bling

Trees

Walking down the hot summer street

That is lined with fruiting orange trees

So ripe and inviting and within arm's reach

A beautiful blessing in a bustling city

That wonderful memory carries me

Across the heat to a colder country

Where the embrace of the willow tree

Stands by the river, nestled locally

As the summer fades away

The sycamore leaves take to the wind to play

After being spread wide, shading and covering

Being parched, falling midseason, then refreshing

Even in the dead of winter

When all the other trees are bare

The evergreen's leaves are still there

Despite the snow, ice and frigid air

From stripped to blooms, from fruit to fall

I've watched a cherry tree do it all

Accompanied by excited little minds

Growing and expanding as the cycle unwinds

There are so many colours to be found in these trees

From browns to reds to oranges and greens

And tones of gold from the oak and its intricate leaves

Scattering its acorns all around

All this resplendence so easily found

Reflections

Looking back upon memories

An era when time seemed to freeze

Almost knocked over by a breeze

That only healing did appease

Now it seems to be smooth sailing

After a rough journey of ups and downs

The destination lies in the waiting

Taking opportunities and making them profound

When the goal used to be

Simply getting through

Now the breath, sweat and tears

Are finally yielding their fruit

Old chapters from the past

Have received a definite closing

Day by day finding reason to last

And reach the well-being of mending

Complex relationships now show signs of health

Evolving makes way for fortuity

Which reveal many different layers of wealth

Such as hindsight and organisational communities

There's a glowing sense of pride
For other's accomplishments too
And the struggles I had to hide
That were overcome before anyone knew

This story has travelled
From adolescence to young adult
This era has ended, a new one has begun
For all the twists and turns
Resilience is the result

THE END